THE SONG OF L

CHRISTOPHER REID

The Song of Lunch

faber and faber

First published in 2009
by CB editions
Published in 2010
by Faber and Faber Ltd
Bloomsbury House
74–77 Great Russell Street
London WC1B 3DA

Typeset by CB editions
Printed in England by CPI Bookmarque, Croydon

A CIP record for this book
is available from the British Library

ISBN 978-0-571-27352-2

10 9 8 7 6 5 4 3 2 1

THE SONG OF LUNCH

HE leaves a message, a yellow sticky,
on the dead black
of his computer screen:
GONE TO LUNCH. I MAY BE SOME TIME.

His colleagues won't be seeing him
for the rest of the afternoon.
Rare joy of truancy, of bold escape
from the trap of work!

That heap of typescript can be left to dwell
on its thousand offences
against grammar and good sense;
his trusty blue pen
can snooze with its cap on;
nobody will notice.

He shuts the door on the sleeping dog
of his own departure,
hurries not too fast along the corridor,
taps the lift button, and waits.

To meet even one person
at this delicate juncture
would sully the whole enterprise.
But he's in luck:
the lift yawns emptily,
he steps in, is enclosed
and carried downwards
to sunlight and London's
approximation of fresh air.

With one bound he is free!

*I*T's a district of literary ghosts
that walk in broad daylight.

Keep your imagination peeled and see
Virginia Woolf
loping off to the library
with a trug full of books.
At every twentieth step,
she takes a sharp drag at a cigarette
and pulls a tormented face
as if she had never tasted anything
so disgusting.

And there goes T. S. Eliot,
bound for his first martini of the day.
With his gig-lamps and his immaculate sheen,
he eases past you like a limousine:
a powerful American model.

Bloomsbury and its blue plaques.
The squares and stucco terraces,
where the little industrious publishers
still like to hide their offices.

Leafy, literary land,
that by some dispensation
has been left to stand
amid the road drills and high, swivelling cranes.

*A*T fifty, he favours a younger man's
impatient pace,
skipping round dawdling
or stupidly halted pedestrians,
doing dares with taxis and trucks.

You're not properly living in London,
if you don't use the dodges, the short cuts.

Yet it's twenty minutes' walk
from work to this lunchtime date
with an old flame.
Gaggles of tourists straggle
more provocatively than ever;
the approach to Bedford Square is blocked:
orange plastic barriers –
our century's major contribution
to the junk art of street furniture!

Never mind, he's making good time –
note the active verb –
and he expects she'll be late.
So he allows himself to feel
pleasure in his own fleetness,
in not being carried but riding
the currents and eddies
of the human torrent.

And occasionally stopping
to let another pass,
unthanked politeness being
the ultimate gesture
of the metropolitan dandy.

*T*HE restaurant
is an old haunt,
though he hasn't been there for years;
not since the publishing trade,
once the province
of swashbucklers and buccaneers,
was waylaid by suits and calculators,
and a strict afternoon
curfew imposed.

Farewell to long lunches
and other boozy pursuits!
Hail to the new age
of the desk potato,
strict hours of imprisonment
and eyesight tortured
by an impassive electronic screen!

Sometimes, though, a man needs
to go out on the rampage,
throw conscientious time-keeping
to the winds,
help kill a few bottles –
and bugger the consequences.
If not a right, exactly,
it's a rite,
and therefore approved in the sight
of some notional higher authority.

*L*UNCH being a game with few rules,
and those unwritten,
it's important to him that the field of play
remain the same
as he fondly remembers it.

Zanzotti's: unreformed Soho Italian.
Chianti-in-a-basket.
Breadsticks you snap
with a sneeze of dust.
Red gingham cloths overlaid
on the diagonal
with plain green paper ones.
Finger smears at the neck
of the water carafe.
And Massimo himself
touring the tables
with his fake bonhomie.

But Soho itself has changed,
the speciality food shops
pushed out of business,
tarts chased off the streets,
and a new kind of trashiness
moving in:
cultureless, fly-by-night.

He stops for a scrawny lad
wheeling a big, unsteady,
rust-patched, festering bin
to park at the roadside,
and wonders what he will find.

*A*ND that's where Dylan Thomas
scrounged ten bob off him,
then set about seducing his girl.

Not.

Seriously, though,
what will they say when they look back
at our demythologised age?

Postmodern Times:
garrulous, garish classic
starring

some idiot off the box.

Charlie Cretin!
Needs work.

Craplin? Forget it.

He cuts down Meard Street,
now much too smart for its name
but where he remembers
a knocking-shop he never went into –
feral whores at the window –
turns the corner, crosses,
and hey presto:
Zanzotti's edges into view.

Exactly as memory has preserved it.

Phew.

Same tricolore paintwork,
thick from repeated coats
and somehow suggesting edibility.

Same signwriter's cursive
festooning the fascia-board
and flanked by the same brass lamps.

It's so much the same, it almost
looks like a replica.

The Wardour Street wideboys and creatives
must love it,
must think it's the campest retro –
when it's the real thing.

Through a gap in the blind,
he can see quite a few of them in there already.
Well, never mind.

He wishes no one ill.

Democracy of the feeding-trough;
swill and let swill.

$\mathcal{H}$E has his hand on the door-handle,
and foot on the grooved step,
when he suddenly recollects –
what, precisely?

Déjà vu? Some artistic analogy?

A true liminal moment,
or simply a trick
of the dictionary-picker's skittering brain?

Eye-corner glimpse
of fugitive epiphany
that, for several beats,
he pursues in vain.

Too bad. Let it go.

He has his hand still on the dimpled
brass bulb of the door-handle.

*W*HICH he turns, noticing
the familiar loose-jointedness:
that's a promising sign.

With the meekest bump of resistance
from the spring contraption overhead,
the door yields and he steps inside
to stand on the prickled mat,
peering into the gloom.

Midday twilight,
requiring adjustment
of all the senses
before it delivers its secrets.

He scans the room,
which is deeper than you might guess from the street,
registers its busyness,
and wonders which of the few
untaken covers will be his.
Not that one by the door
to the toilets, he hopes;
nor the one with too much window light.
Snug privacy is what he wants:
to be tucked away from the bustle:
ideally, over there.

On the threshold, on the edge
of a shadow-world
that is yet to welcome him,
he stands and waits

Waits for a waiter

*F*IRST disappointing thing:
no sign of Massimo,
nor of his old staff –
Massimo's pirate crew,
as he privately thought of them;
some of whose names he knew
while knowing nothing of their lives
beyond the act –
grave, flirtatious,
resentful, brisk, droll –
each brought to the table.

Instead, young men and women –
roughly half-and-half –
and not all looking
especially Italian.

How long has it been?
Five years? Six years?
Ten?

Fifteen?

God help us all.

Though Time's wingèd chariot
with the brakes off and in full
downhill hurtle
must be inaudible –
unheard-of, rather –
to these sprightly boys and girls.

*H*E is noticed but not recognised
by a waiter he does not recognise,
but who catches his name
in his right ear, then bows
clerically over the ledger
that bulges from all the names,
the months and years of names,
written in it,
and that sits open on a slope
like a church-lectern bible.
The Book of Reservations.

As ever, that pause
of anxiety and mute appeal.
But there, happily, it is:
scriptural confirmation.
Without a smile, without a word,
he is eyebrowed and nodded to follow.

Which he does, past tables,
past people at tables,
he is careful not to brush
with either himself or his shoulder-bag.

Aloof carriage, side-steps,
calculated indirection:
it's as much a dance as a walk.

And it gets him nicely
to the spot he had spotted
from the door.
Laid for two. A little island. An eyot.
Perfect.

MENU, thank you.
And wine list?

On the back. I see.

So things are different after all:
under new mismanagement.

Might have known it.
(Did know it perhaps?)

The very table linen
has lost its patriotism.
Plain white: we surrender.

And this menu, this twanging
laminated card,
big as a riot policeman's shield?

Hm, at first glance,
pizzas by the yard.
More pizzas than there should be.
And too much designer pizazz.

He turns it over:
choose the right wine
and have it ready breathing
for when she arrives.

There's a mid-price Chianti,
which won't come plump
in tight straw swaddling,
but will do for auld lang syne.

Old time's sake
being the precarious purpose
of this tête-à-tête

and possibly
a great big mistake.

WE said we wouldn't look back.

Innocent jaunty wistful
ditty from some old musical
trips from the wings
and would run uninterrupted
if he didn't shoo it away.

Just one of those things.
Ditto.

A song for every cliché!

Though it was more, he's perfectly sure,
than a bell that now and then

Why did she e-mail him
suggesting

No, he

Woofs of laughter
in imprecise unison
from a table, all men,
jolly good company,
off to his right.

He draws a breadstick,
wrong brand, from its ripped sheath
and beheads it with a bite.

*I*N twilight himself
he commands, nice word,
a clear view of the entrance,
lit contre-jour
so that each new arrival
new candidate for his notice
appears to step
from brightness to bathos
with a tacit apology:
Sorry, I'm not

But if not, what?
What will she look like?

On his third tasteless
but moreish breadstick,
he's startled: she's changed.
But he's wrong. She hasn't. She isn't.

Back to his chewing:
the fragmentation
and mashing of rusk
soothingly loud
in the isolated chamber of his skull.

*F*WOP!
The cork leaves the bottle
and his quick nose
wants to pick up
the escaping bouquet.
Will it be all right?

The waiter pours out
the statutory measure –
one imperial glug –
which he lifts and breathes over
thinkingly. Not corked.
Good. Then sips.
Nods.

That's fine, thank you.
Leave it there please.

He'll do the pouring.

It's quite sharp
but should broaden out.

He takes his tumbler of water,
overweight bubbles
mobbing up to greet him,
sips that and feels
the chill fizz
smash against his palate.
Thirstier than he thought,
he drinks till the ice
rests on his upper lip.

*H*ELLO?

He jolts. Ice cubes
slurrily clatter
to the bottom of the tumbler
as he bumps it back on the table.
Wiping his wet lip
also expresses surprise.

She's here. How did that happen!
Had he taken his eyes
off the door for so long?

Flustered, self-reprimanding,
he is still able to start to rise
from his seat with a greeting smile

Well, hello. I didn't see

and be met half-way
with a soft peck
smack in the middle of his mouth.
Familiar collision
of pout against pout
though there's something different too.
A new: what? Fragrance? Aura?
Hint of carefree expenditure?
Waft of wealth?

How lovely.

I hope I'm not late.

You're not late at all.

*S*o: the human paradox:
the same and changed.
All that he remembers
vivid in the differences.

Is she thinner?
Somehow there's a sharper outline
which is not just smart tailoring;
and her hair looks better behaved.

She hangs her bag,
pampered scarlet leather,
over the back of her chair
and skips into the seat.
Now! that movement says –
quick, eager, a touch needy,
as if she were beginning a lesson
in a subject she's good at.
It puts him on his mettle.

There! she says, and smiles.
Lips, eyes, eyebrows
and the new lines in her forehead
fill out the harmony.

Here! he replies.

HAVE some wine, he adds,
any stage business
being better than a dry.
I'm afraid it hasn't really had time,
but

He pours into the two glasses,
measuring by ear
identical notes,
then doesn't put the bottle down.
He has a speech to deliver.

This is a disappointment.
Remember the old flasks?
Kitsch, I know,
but didn't you have a soft spot?
Snug in their raffia
like fat cuckoos in small nests.
Still, nothing lasts.
What's the toast?

Happy days?

Happy days it is

(looking both ways).

Rims meet and clink
swaying the cradled liquid:
dark, sluggish, ink.

*A*ND they drink.

Becoming palatable.

Her expression expresses no judgement
and she puts the glass down.

You haven't changed.

I have.

Witness this morning's bathroom mirror:
the grey, the flab, the stoop, the frown,
and in the deliberating,
disbelieving eyes
something like terror.

Not to notice.

Was that one of the problems, he wonders:
her blithe rebuffing of such facts
as didn't match
an optimistic outlook?

He could argue

but the waiter intervenes
with a second menu,
which slices into
the infant conversation
like a sweetly-swung axe.

*I*T's almost all pizzas,
he apologises
before she has read a word.
I'm afraid the place has gone to the dogs.

She looks around, cursorily.

Don't be absurd, it's fine;
in fact, at first glance,
it's improved.
To be honest, when you suggested this,
I wasn't so sure.
Almost any other venue.
All that surly waiter business
was much more your kick than mine.
But when I came in the door,
I thought, well, OK.
And I'm quite glad to see a menu
that doesn't make a fetish
of stracciatella and pollo sorpreso.

Good. Excellent. If you say so.

Did he play the wrong card?
Could things be turning nasty?
Retreating to cover,
he concentrates hard
on the antipasti.

ACROSS the table
across clean cloth and clutter
she leans and wooingly twice
with middle finger
nudges him on the knuckle.

Come on, no sulks. Be nice. Sois sage.

Cajoling English and caressing French.

How long has it been?
Ten years? Eleven?

Fifteen.

No, it can't be that,
let's settle for twelve.
And we've only got lunch
in which to tell each other
everything. So
Truce?

For a moment, he withholds,
mouth full of pause,
which he can either spit out or swallow.
What's the use

Pax, he agrees, aggrieved.

And they shake hands,
a squeeze of fingers rather:
hers light then tight
then light again in his,
then efficiently retrieved.

*S*o. Who's to start?

You.

Right.

His glass is drained,
hers is barely touched.
Judiciously, he brings
the levels level.

Right: I'll tell you everything I can
there's little to relate
it was an agèd agèd man

Stop! She looks pained.

What?

Stop. If you can't be serious
we'll talk about something else.
Or nothing at all.

I was about to do that.
That's my whole story.

Signora signore.

Impeccable timing!

Are you ready to order?

We haven't

Yes thank you:
but I'd like some advice.

She doesn't need it,
but it's her style
to entrust herself
in unimportant matters,
pose questions that are easy to answer,
and indeed it makes the waiter smile
when tapping the menu decisively
she requests the pumpkin ravioli
because he has recommended it,
with sea bass to follow.

His turn. Carpaccio.
And – in the absence of pollo
whatsit – a pizza Napoletana,
extra anchovies.

No one smiles at that,
because he is not nice.

*W*HAT say we start again?

Wind back the years?

Minutes. You know what I mean.

Ah, my autobiography:
no change there.
Confessions of a Copy Editor,
chapter 93.
It's an ordinary day
in a publishing house
of ill repute.
Another moronic manuscript
comes crashing down the chute
to be turned into art.
This morning it was Wayne Wanker's
latest dog's dinner
of sex, teenage philosophy
and writing-course prose.
Abracadabra, kick it up the arse –
and out it goes
to be Book of the Week
or some other bollocks.
What a fraud. What a farce.
And tomorrow: who knows
which of our geniuses
will escape from the zoo
and head straight for us
with a new masterpiece
lifeless in his jaws.
That's about the size of it.
What about you?

*B*USINESS as usual, then.

Yes, business as usual.

After such a rant,
he finds it difficult
to look her in the eye:
which is bright amused searching pitiless:
but he has to try.

A sip may help.

When he notices for the first time
the faint, faint
nimbus of the lens
circling the gold-shot
hazel of each iris.
Well, of course.
Oracle eyes
he used to call them:
the harder you looked,
the more sublime
and unreadable they became.
But have they lost their old force?

The heretical question
strengthens his own stare.

Gaze meets gaze,
revealing as ever
everything and nothing there.

*F*LYAWAY thought.

Back to life.

And you?

Me? Oh, the good wife
and loving mother.
That keeps me occupied.
I've no complaints.
And Paris is a fabulous city.
You really should visit.

He has, but is it
the moment to mention
that crazed escapade:
skulking at dusk
in her prim grey square
address folded
in his raincoat pocket
with no real intention
of ringing the doorbell
yet unable to depart
until the horrible
shock of the pigeons
an entire flock
rising at some scare
into the diminished light
like a thousand umbrellas
simultaneously opening
and telling him to go

No, he thinks. No

*H*E is startled from this reckless
plunge into memory
by his own awareness of it:
like snapping out of a doze.
How long can it have lasted?
Gone some time.

But she seems not to have noticed,
averted from him,
twisting in her seat,
chin raised, eyes reconnoitring.

He'd like to kiss her long neck,
nibble it, nuzzle
her jawbone with his nose.

Which one is our waiter?
We could do with some more water.

That's him there.

Are you sure?

You can't have forgotten,
you were practically seducing him
a minute ago.

She swivels her gaze back:
smiling, surprisingly.

It's nice to know
you're still madly jealous.

Oh yes, he's rotten with jealousy.

Absolutely I am not.
But now we're on the subject –
how is the old pseud?

He means her husband,
the celebrated novelist.
She throws out a laugh:
a single syllable
and its full stop.

Flourishing, thank you.

The ubiquitous jacket photo.
The wintry smirk
that stole her from him.

How could she have been so gullible?

There's a new book of stories
out in the autumn,
and right now he's hard at work
on some lectures that Harvard
have asked him to do.
So everything's perfect.

And how could he
have been so abject
as to let it happen?

ONCE more she is distracted,
catching the eye of the waiter
with a demure flutter
of restaurant semaphore
and asking for more water.

And we'll need another
bottle of this.

The waiter goes:
one of those fellows
you'd describe as nondescript
if the word wasn't forbidden.
How many times
in some author's manuscript
has he crossed it out and written
There is nothing that cannot be described.
But in this particular case,
searching in vain
for any distinctive feature,
he may allow an exception.

*F*ROM that thought idly
on a ride of the eye
around the room –
the bustle, the hubbub –
he travels to the next:
a small dark waitress carrying
three filled plates
from the kitchen hatch
reverses pauses turns proceeds
with such practised fluency
that he'd like to catch
her eye to show her
his appreciation
and be rewarded
by her appreciation of his

but away she speeds

*H*IS absentee mind
squirrels back to immediate matters.

He utters a cough,
curt, formal,
an otiose throat-clear.

Right.

Does he
Does he know that we're

Having lunch?

Yes.
Of course. I told him.
And he instructed me to pass on
his warmest regards.
Which I've no intention of doing.
As he well knows.

That's very kind. Of both of you.
I suppose.

ACCORDING to established rites,
wine and water are brought
with less ceremony than before.
There are no fresh glasses
and the waiter does not pour
a specimen measure.
But the first courses
arrive soon after –
ravioli anointed with butter,
carpaccio with a chrism of oil –
and the condiments are distributed:
parmesan shaved
from a nubbly, fulvous block,
a sesquipedalian peppermill waved
by the nimble attendant of the kitchen hatch
in final blessing.
He watches, and his companion
watches him watch,
the flexing of supple back
and sturdy haunches
as the waitress raises
and twists the head
of the wooden phallus,
scattering seed.

They scarcely need
the waiter's intoned
Buon appetito.

*F*IRST mouthfuls are discussed
and pronounced delicious.
Then, as of old,
forks trade between dishes
and swaps are analysed.

Mmmn. You chose well.
Nutmeg I think. Or could it be mace?

Beef's beautifully lean;
and the capers are not too overpowering.

Moist and light:
you can tell it was made
barely a minute ago.

Sweet accord
of comparisons and compliments
recalling a time
before the souring.

I suppose this is nothing
to what you're used to.

Paris? You know, we never eat out.
I'm a slave to the kitchen stove.
The boys have appetites
but absolutely no taste.
It's like feeding large dogs.
Smart restaurants, haute cuisine,
would be a total waste.
So this, even Zanzotti's,
is a rare treat.

Despite the qualification,
satisfying to hear.

*H*E has killed a bottle
almost singlehanded.
When he seizes the new one
and nods it in her direction,
her flattened hand
places an interdiction
on the half-full glass
that would be half-empty to him.

Slender fingers
once so intimate
and versatile and tender.
Whorls of wrinkles
sealing the knuckles
deeper now,
though the lacquerless nails
remain buffed and neat.

Admitting defeat,
the bottle withdraws
backwards still bowing
like a courtier,
turns to his own glass
and

A word in your ear

blurts out its sorrows
in a splashy gabble.

WITH the blade of her fork
she presses down
punctures gashes
saws seesaws
slices in two
a plump glistening
pasta packet
then scoops and carries
half to her mouth.

Chews.

Chews, he observes,
with less conspicuous relish
than she used to.

Have all her appetites
turned less lusty?

Mind your own business.

*B*UT isn't it his business
to remember certain times

old times
bedtimes
betweentimes
anytimes

of a startling impromptu
innocent lasciviousness

that he'll never know again?

Sleep-musky kisses
that roused him in the small hours

Peremptory custody
of light firm limbs

The polyrhythmic riding

he'll never know again

CAUGHT a fish and let it go
woe woe woe woe

Whoops and jeers
from the table of blokes.
More ragged this time
and prolonged,
their laughter issues
richly from fed bellies
and lubricated throats.
The lads who lunch.

Found a treasure and threw it away
hey hey

Drop it now

But jaws rending the raw meat
beat beat beat beat
a relentless measure.

Audible, fortunately,
only to himself.

FIGURE of folly and pathos:
voyeur of the past.

And of the present. He steals a peep.

Finished ahead of him, she settles her fork
at six o'clock,
takes a sip of wine, then a rinse of water,
and mops her mouth with her napkin:
four dabs, right to left.

Every movement
has elegance and economy,
is swift and deft.

The jut of her wristbone,
marvel of engineering,
holds the secret,
and as a connoisseur
he yearns to inspect it
at closer quarters,
by eye and by touch.
But how can he catch it?

Like a butterfly-hunter,
he ponders the problem.

Sweetheart, she whispers,
I hate to say it, but you're leering.

$\mathcal{M}$Y god. You're right. I'm sorry.
It's the old male gaze

(through alcoholic haze)

You can say that again.

I was falling in love with your wrist.
I think I've become
a wrist festishist.

You're an everything fetishist,
always have been.

Guilty.

You know, it's one thing to ogle
a waitress's bum,
but this is the wrist of a married woman.

She raises an arm;
sleeve-cuff and bangles
shuffle down;
bone bump stands prominent;
faint blue veins show to the fore.

Private property. Look.
I'm sure you can see
the mark of the manacles.
So kindly desist.
Now, where are the toilets?

Up and off
forgoing reply
she mazes her way to the door.

$\mathcal{H}$E glooms at his glass.
Forefinger linking stem,
he lifts it, gives the wine
an indolent, anticlockwise swirl,
then lowers it again to the cloth.
Half-empty. But that can wait.
How's the bottle? Plenty.

He thinks. Thinks about drink,
about his drinking.
The taste of his last mouthful
lies like rust on his tongue:
harsh: and yet his tongue craves more.
At rest in the glass, the wine is rusted purple.
So there exists an affinity, a strong
mutual pull
between wine and tongue.
They are complementary.
They are in love.
The silent tongue calls out, and the wine,
though inanimate,
will heed the call.

Well, it's a theory: lent support
when the glass rises and this time
not stopping short
delivers one lover to the other.
They kiss;
there's a little death:
an insufficient bliss,
but repeatable later.

HA! That's one thing that hasn't improved.

Still the same old?

Same old. Medieval.

I can't wait to see the Gents.

I'm sure you won't be disappointed.

All at once the whole of Soho,
its acres of cottage architecture,
presents itself to his vision:
a hidden system
of steep, narrow,
listing staircases
and ever dimmer and dingier
zigzag passageways,
squeezed in as tight as intestines.
Proliferation of doors marked PRIVATE,
with hellhole kitchens behind them:
hobs aflame, pots on perpetual simmer.
And at the end of each lonely quest,
that more public private room
frankly, rankly announcing its function.
Yet all somehow beautiful and right;
all making perfect sense
to the true scholar
of secrecy and squalor.
Someone should write
Perhaps

But he's interrupted by mention
of a book he's actually written.
His own. His only.

*N*o. Blow-all. Not a squeak.

True. The Muse of Misery,
so lavish in her attentions
for a year or two,
has not revisited,
and that modest volume of thirty-six
wounded and weeping lyrics
remains unique.

Not that the world cries out for more.
One shitty review in the TLS –
The poetry, we assume,
is in the self-pity –
earned its round of common-room sniggers
and put the dampers on that.
Sales scraped through to three figures
and the once gung-ho publisher
ceased to return phone-calls.

An illuminating history of betrayals!

The book conceived in tears
will be born drowned.

*T*HAT's a great shame.
Naturally, I wasn't your most
objective reader,
but I thought the poems had real power.
Some of the mythic stuff was over the top,
but I could see your
our

Stop right there! What do you mean,
mythic stuff? The mythic stuff
was the whole fucking point

Well, for a start,
I'm not actually in thrall
to the King of Death.
Or whoever he's meant to be.

But you are – don't you see?

And you're totally Orpheus

Right.

And I'm

You're my wife, you're dead,
and it's my business to bring you back to life.
Which I very nearly succeed in doing

But you don't. No way.
Because I like being dead.
And that's where the metaphor
the analogy
the whole preposterous contrivance
falls apart.

*S*o you loathed it.

I had my quibbles.

You loathed it.

No.

Pause, for second courses
to come alongside.

It's the little dark agile waitress,
the athlete–ballerina
with her deadpan demeanour,
who serves them both.
Refusal to smile
explains her style.

That and heavy black eyebrows.

Sea bass for the signora

Thank you

and for him
a wheel of gloop-smothered dough
singed at the rim.

He stares, wonders why, remembers,
accepts pepper – for the performance –
refuses cheese,
then with knife and fork
carves an uneven wedge
from the charred edge,
lifts, inspects, nibbles.

No swaps this time
though the sea bass looks a treat:
scorch-glistered skin
peeled back laboratory-fashion
from the moist grey savoury meat.
Head with stunned amber eyes
severed and pushed to one side.

Conversation on hold,
the scuffle and clack
of her cutlery
send out signals
not difficult to interpret.

But he's soothed by the ambient blah:
the big white noise
of a room that's full
of anonymously feeding humans.
Even the too-near table
of boisterous boys
contributes to its euphony,
its equilibrium.
There is peace
at the heart of the din,
concord in babel.

Then a kick on the shin

*T*HIS is ground control. Can you hear me?

Loud and clear.

I seem to have hurt your feelings.

Not at all.
I've had my feelings
surgically removed.
They can't be touched by anyone now.

Oh my dear

She stretches, touches
the back of his hand.
He cannot not feel
her middle finger
lightly and with calm,
rotatory strokes
massage behind his knuckles,
then her thumb shove
into his fist
and nuzzle against his palm.

The strokes continue.

*J*UST what he doesn't want:
the untimely stirring
of what could become
by not so slow degrees
a major bonk.

Not now, please

It's like an old tired
foolishly friendly
mostly forgotten dog
that's chosen an awkward moment
to rouse and shake itself
from its basket
and demand a romp.

Down, boy, down

(thank you, Robert Graves)

Down, I said

And he can't be sure if it's willpower
or the wine
but the dog reluctantly behaves,
retreating to its lonesome, malodorous nest
for another long nap.

Good chap

Good chap

*T*HANK you, nurse, the agony
is quite abated.

Her hand withdraws.

Pause, followed
by another pause.

He surveys the dismaying
landscape of his pizza.

She's done better.

Half her fish cleanly eaten,
with the point of her knife
she loosens the backbone
from the underlying flesh,
prises it clear,
shakes till the neck-end
detaches from the rest
taking a few shreds with it,
and lays the skeleton –
bones graded
like a primitive musical instrument,
plucked or struck –
on the side of her dish.

*S*URPRISE idea:
culinary porn!

If it hasn't been done already

All tastes catered for

Elegant dismemberment
of succulent morsels
by the fetish mistress

as here

Or for those who prefer it
rough and rude

women wrestling in fast food!

Must be some establishment close by
where

*P*ENNY?

Sorry?

Your thoughts.

No. I wasn't thinking, exactly.
More probing a mental dimension
beyond time and space

Typical! You can't even pay attention
for the few minutes we have.
I've come all this way,
dropped my family
at not the most convenient moment,
hopped on the Shuttle,
taken the taxi ride from hell,
convinced at every traffic light I'd be late,
and here I am, all tuned up for our little reunion,
only to find
your physical, guzzling, tippling self
recognisably present,
but your mind
appears to have flitted off on holiday.
You're out to lunch at your own lunch!

That's nicely put
and no doubt true as well.
The sort of thing they used to say
on my school report.
Along with unteachable and half-witted.
Guzzling's unfair, though:
I really can't manage
the rest of this.

TIPPLING, however

He lifts, tilts, gulps.

I take it you're

Refills own. Not a lot left

Antidote to all life's ills!

Another gulp.

Are there so many?

Ha! Funny!

I wasn't trying to be

I suppose, in number, not many

That's reassuring.

Just one big

Then, master of ceremonies:

Drink to me only!

Swig.

Seems to help.

I APPEAR to have lost my appetite as well.

Knife and fork conjoin primly.

You'll leave a fishy
half a fishy
Sad waste

She wipes untainted fingers,
mops and licks lips.

Borrow a taste?
Better not

This hasn't gone quite as I expected.

How did you expect?

Blank.

It to go

Oh I don't know:
more of the old
Whatever we had
Which wasn't bad,
was it? We did have fun,
didn't we?

We did

Di da da da

And no harm done.
Till the King of Death arrived on the scene.

Or should I say the King of Prose?

Or should you say nothing
One minute
Yes, thank you

The waiter nods:
a minimal bow
of assent/enquiry.

and I believe my friend
has finished with his.

Plates, cutlery, leavings of food
are flourished away
to be shelved on a forearm.

Dessert? Coffee?

Her no to both.

Dully he concurs
till an idea glows

glows and grows
in the murk of his brain

fine fiery
feisty candle-flame:

But I think I could handle
a little grappa

*U*N grappino. Sì, signore.

And away he zooms
on waiter business

waiter among waiters
zapping and arabesquing
from table to table
like bees between blooms

business and buzziness

now that busy waitress
the bee ballerina
is she sting or is she sweetness

nowhere to be seen

*W*HERE are you this time?

God, I'm sorry

Sorry indeed.
I hadn't expected you
to have gone to seed
with quite such abandon.
Or is this some sort of
cock-eyed performance
you're putting on for my special benefit?

I think I need
to think about that one.

Right. Well,
while you're doing that,
I'll tell you what I think.

$\mathcal{F}$OR which we need to go back to your poems.
It strikes me you don't understand them yourself.
They're not about me. I wasn't the kidnap victim;
it was you who were snatched and carried away
to some region of darkness by — oh, by let's call her
the Queen of the Fairies. Don't interrupt:
I'm finding the words as I go along,
but when I've stopped, we'll see if the theory's
up to scrutiny. Now, according to my logic,
the Eurydice that you're trying to rescue
with your brave little song must be yourself:
your inner self, your soul. But you've not been in touch
with that in your entire life. Which puts you in a hole,
strategically speaking. And who was it dumped you there
in the first place? The kidnapper I was talking about,
whom I can now reveal to be
the Lyric Muse: who should have left you alone
to work out your problems in some healthier fashion
and not led you on, not made you confuse
poetry with therapy. And who's also to blame
for your present state of emotional arrest,
infantile truculence and drunken flippancy.
It's not just that you're stuck in the past,
you're stuck in your poems. Which have their merits:
they're nicely written, they're clever, and so on.
But they're misconceived, false, hollow, wrong.
You should never have gone there. Yet you did.
That's the catastrophe. That's the disaster.

*Y*ou're going to have to repeat that
I want to write it down
especially the bit about flippulant, yes
what
I'm perfectly serious

Ever the escape artist,
ever the clown

The oracle eyes
appear to have tears in them
but too proud to fall

No, I'm sure you're right.

Nip of grappa,
distillation of grape-pips,
sits on the tongue a moment
transmitting warmth
to the outer limbs
then slips to its doom.

My little book was a great big
bag of shite;
when I thought I was writing hymns
to your sublime beauty
and our lost love.
Thank you for the elucidation.
Now, if you'll excuse me,
I must find my way to the little girls'
sorry, not funny
little boys' room.

*T*HE big noisy boys are getting up to leave,
so he chooses a roundabout route,
taking care
from a safe but visible distance
to throw them a killer glare.
One of them catches it, baffled.

Customers are thinning out,
and he's glad of the assistance
of an empty table
when he negotiates a corner
and the floor sways.

Last leg to the labelled door
is straightforward, however,
and he's through it without mishap.
So far so clever

The Gents – he doesn't need the arrow –
is along the passage
and down some narrow steps
that tip him in
faster than calculated.
But he's made it: knows at once
the old chemical fragrance
which only partially smothers
the jabbing kidney reek
that proclaims all men brothers.

And there's the familiar
porcelain trough
with its ancient stains
and crazed glaze.

*I*T is while he is standing
watching his yellow stream
slither sluggishly
away along the gully
that he conceives his scheme:
to find the dark-browed waitress
to find her and?
ask her to marry him!

Once out the door
and up the short flight
turn left not right
past the Ladies
then left again
down a doorless corridor
with at the end a longer flight
to a windowed half-landing
view of brickwork and drainpipes
turn about and aided by shaky handrail
up to the first floor
two doors both rattled both locked
then up up up by steeper steps
and odder odours
to the very top:
two doors again: again locked
again unanswered.

He sits on the highest step.
An erupting pigeon briefly interrupts
the slant view
through that half-landing window.
Otherwise: silence, non-event.

Now he can't decide
whether to weep or sleep

$\mathcal{H}$E is woken up by somebody
waking up inside him
abruptly and roughly.
After some seconds' ugly tussle
he identifies his assailant
as himself,
they reach an agreement,
encourage each other to consciousness
and become one.

What is he doing
crouched on this high shelf?

The brick view
illuminates nothing,
but a wheedling smell
mixture of kitchen wafts
and structural mildew
helps him to recall
Lunch, oh
and grappling the handrail
to clamber to his feet.

Nicely judged
lurches propel him
down to the ground floor
and a more stately progress
just once cannoning off the wall
brings him back to the restaurant
now almost deserted

That's his table over there:
unoccupied

*L*ESS than an hour has passed
but he might have died
and be returning as a ghost.

A waiter not the same one

non–nondescript!

intercepts him swiftly,
draws him aside:

The lady she go.
You no come back. She pay.

Airy hesitation:
he tucks his wallet away.

Was she
Was she angry?

Big shrug. Big shake of head.
Comical, big-mouthed grimace.

Wouldn't care to say
same as enough said.

Look: they've looked after his shoulder-bag.

Thank you.

He produces a tip
the size of which surprises him.

Now he is saddled
and ready to depart.

But first, a last
goodbye to the old place.

Nothing more empty
than a room full of tables
laid but without occupants

No, wait: there's someone
seated by the window:
a very old man:
parchment face,
sparse white hairs
combed in strict parallels,
blind staring eyes,
black tie, black suit,
rigid as a cadaver
from some Sicilian catacomb.

Husk of life
without sap, without savour

Nudge him, he'll crumble

$\mathcal{A}$s he turns to go
the recognition pierces him:

Massimo!